GYM TALES & BARBELLS

BELLA'S JOURNEY

BY JUSTIN MORRISSETTE

XULON PRESS

Xulon Press
2301 Lucien Way #415
Maitland, FL 32751
407.339.4217
www.xulonpress.com

Paperback ISBN-13: 978-1-66280-555-4

Ebook ISBN-13: 978-1-6628-0556-1

To everyone who is trying to find their purpose in life - this one is for you! Thank you to my wife, Kendra, for all of your love and support and to Averi Lain for your illustration inspiration.

Bella is a new barbell at the gym. She is excited to get going!

"Barbells, get ready!"
says Baxter the barbell.

The class is full of advanced athletes.

Bella is excited to do her first workout!

The class starts to pick out barbells.

All of the barbells get chosen
one by one...except Bella.

The class finishes their workout and puts their equipment away. "This is unfair!" shouts Bella.

"Bella, why are you sad?" asks Baxter. "I'm sad because I didn't get picked for the workout. I wish I was a bigger barbell ... like you." says Bella.

"You are made for a unique purpose, Bella. You can help new athletes feel comfortable with a barbell because you are lighter!" says Baxter.

The beginner class is about to start. They are working on overhead presses today!
After the warm-up, they begin picking out barbells.

Bella gets picked!

She is happy to be chosen.

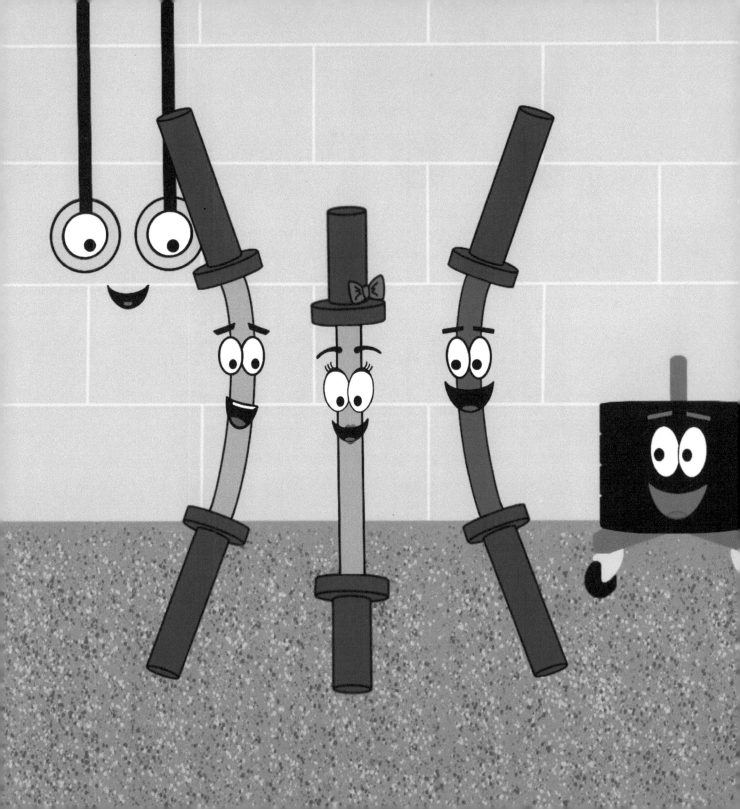

"I guess it's not so bad being a small barbell after all! I have been created to fulfill a unique purpose."

CPSIA information can be obtained
at www.ICGtesting.com
Printed in the USA
BVHW051516220421
605631BV00009B/394